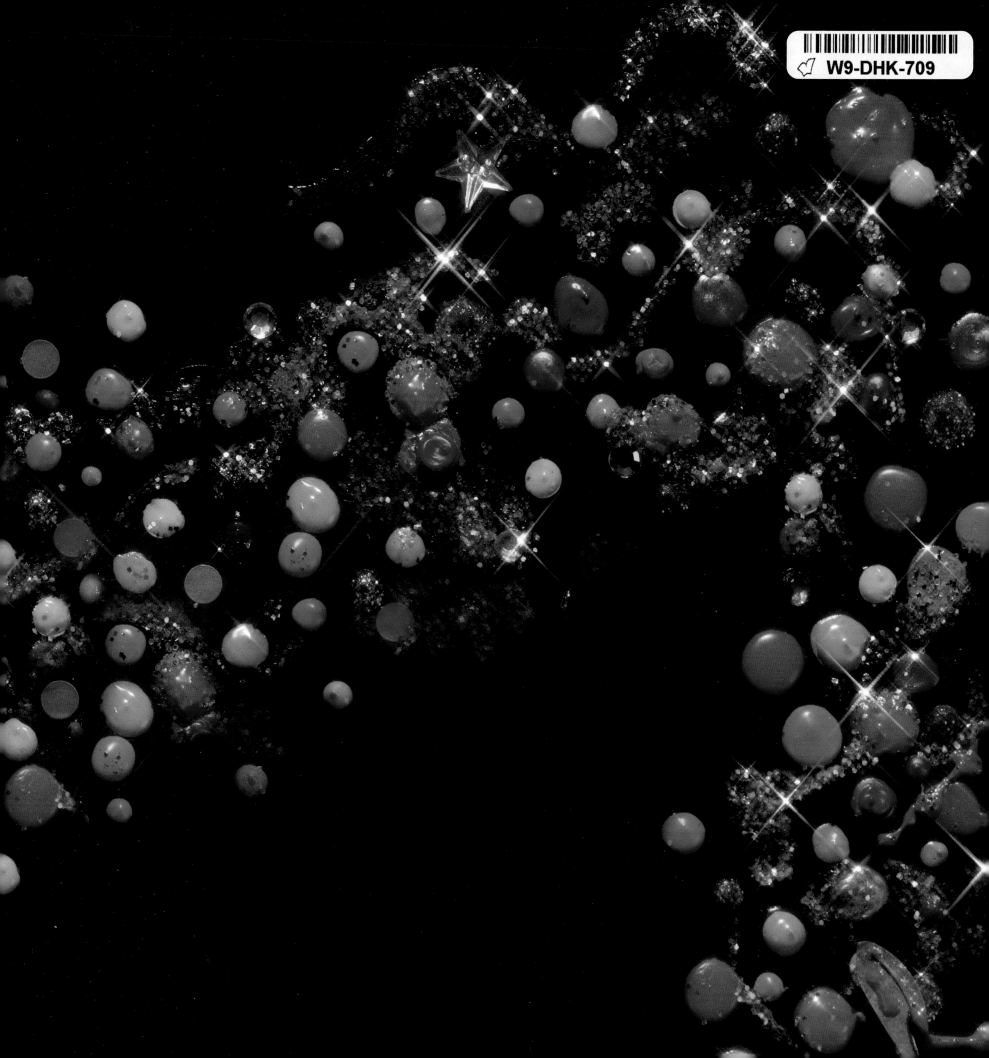

The Zebra-Striped Whale with the Polka-Dot Tail

Inspired by Leon Leigh Faden

Verse and Art by
Shari Faden Donahue

ARIMAX, INC.
Post Office Box 53
Washington Crossing, Pennsylvania 18977
E-mail: Arimax1@aol.com
www.arimaxkids.com

Original hand-scripted initial caps by Maxime Chandis Donahue.
Original end paper spiral tissue collage by Ariele Jacquel Donahue.

Afterword quote by Leon Leigh Faden excerpted from his original poem,
How Precious, Your Loving Kindness.

Consultants: Thomas William Donahue, Shelley Faden Focht

Library of Congress Catalog Card Number: 98-93673
ISBN: 0-9634287-3-X
Printed in Hong Kong
Second Printing 2001

Maxime and Ariele ~

Your precious gifts of love and inspiration

have set me asail

on a truly magical trail!

Tom ~

I am grateful that, together, we share

the wonders of life's journey.

Bec ~

You have taught me to go the extra mile,

to ask questions, to seek honest answers,

and to value integrity, Mom;

thanks for lighting my steps with your wisdom.

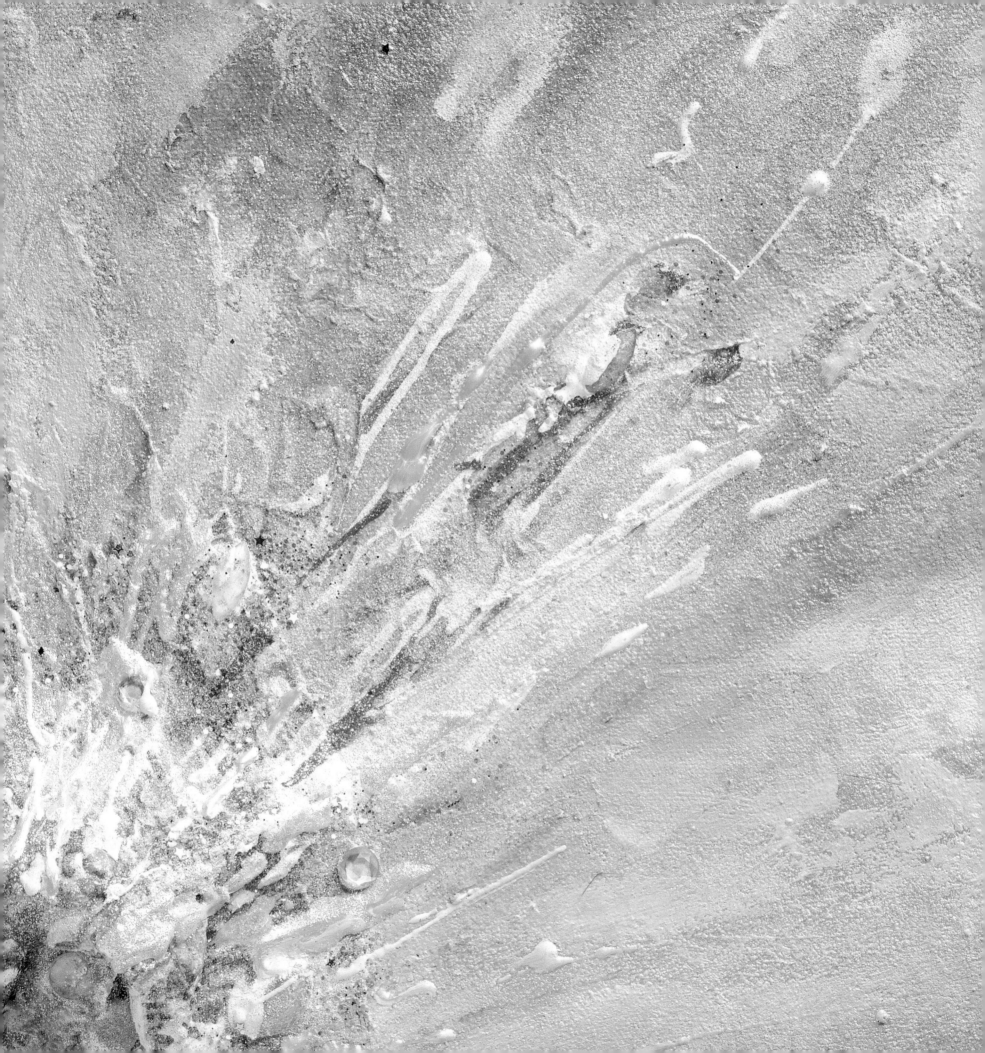

I

rejoice

in the warm glow

kindled by the memory of my father

LEON LEIGH FADEN

precious gift of love

embracing my spirit, soothing my soul

lighting my path

to life's brilliant colors

"Wow," exclaims Maxime.
"Hey, look at that whale!
It has a zebra-striped body
And a polka-dot tail!"

"I see it," says Ariele,
With her mouth open wide.
"A pink and purple octopus
Swims right by her side!"

They look down for a moment,
And right within reach…
Is a gloriously glimmering,
Shimmering beach!

The colors of the rainbow
Light each granule of sand.
"Amazing!" screams Maxime
As she grabs Ariele's hand.

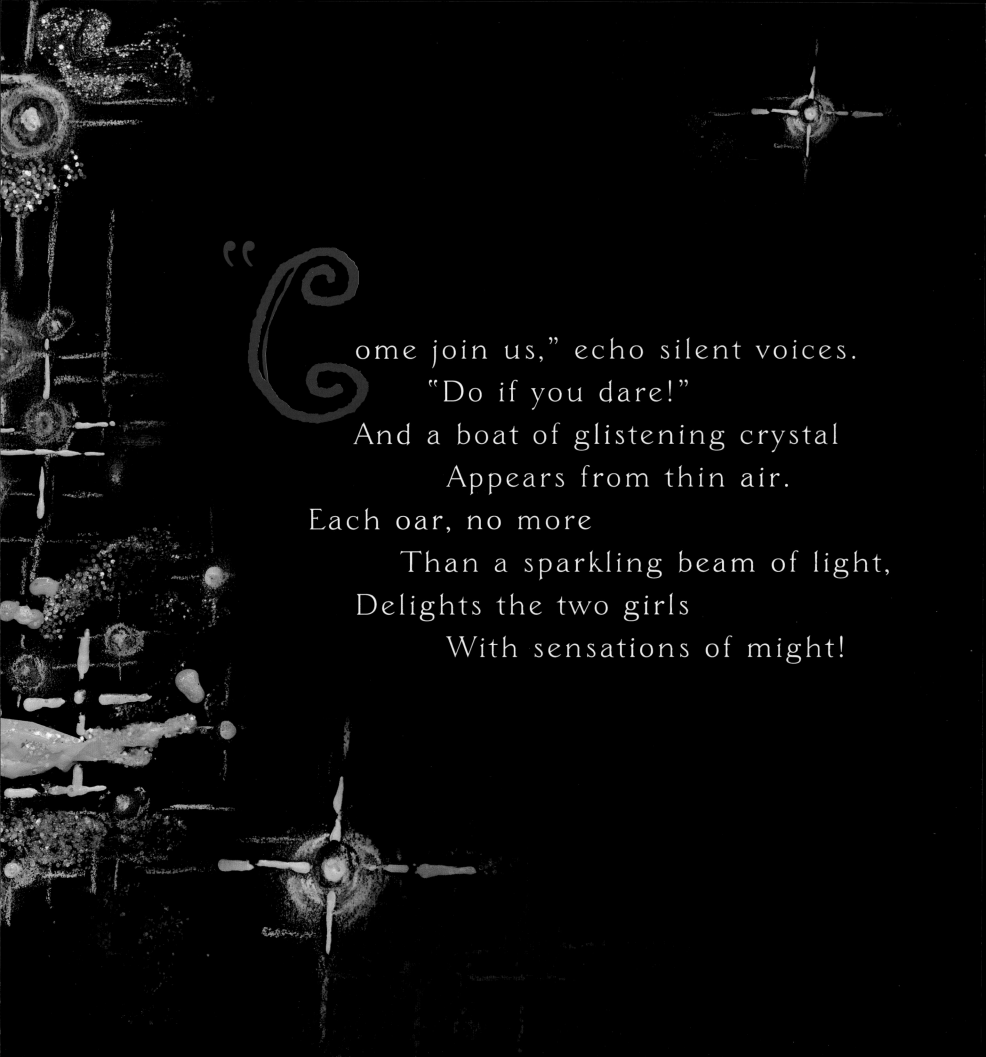

"Come join us," echo silent voices.
　　"Do if you dare!"
And a boat of glistening crystal
　　Appears from thin air.
Each oar, no more
　　Than a sparkling beam of light,
Delights the two girls
　　With sensations of might!

They boldly step in…
        Begin to wildly spin…
Sparkles erupt
        In a tremendous whirlwind!

The octopus waves her arms.
The whale rattles her tail.
Polka dots are unleashed
In a magical trail!

Spiraling higher

and higher, they approach a space known to few...

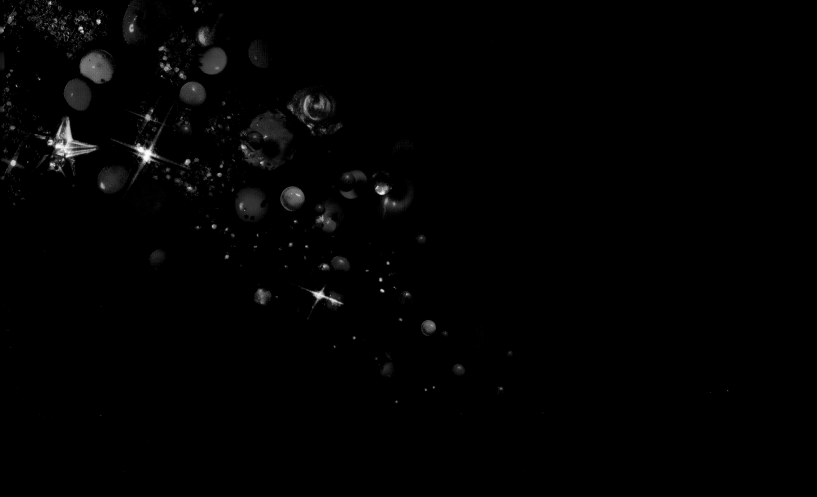

Where all trues are FALSE

And all falses are TRUE

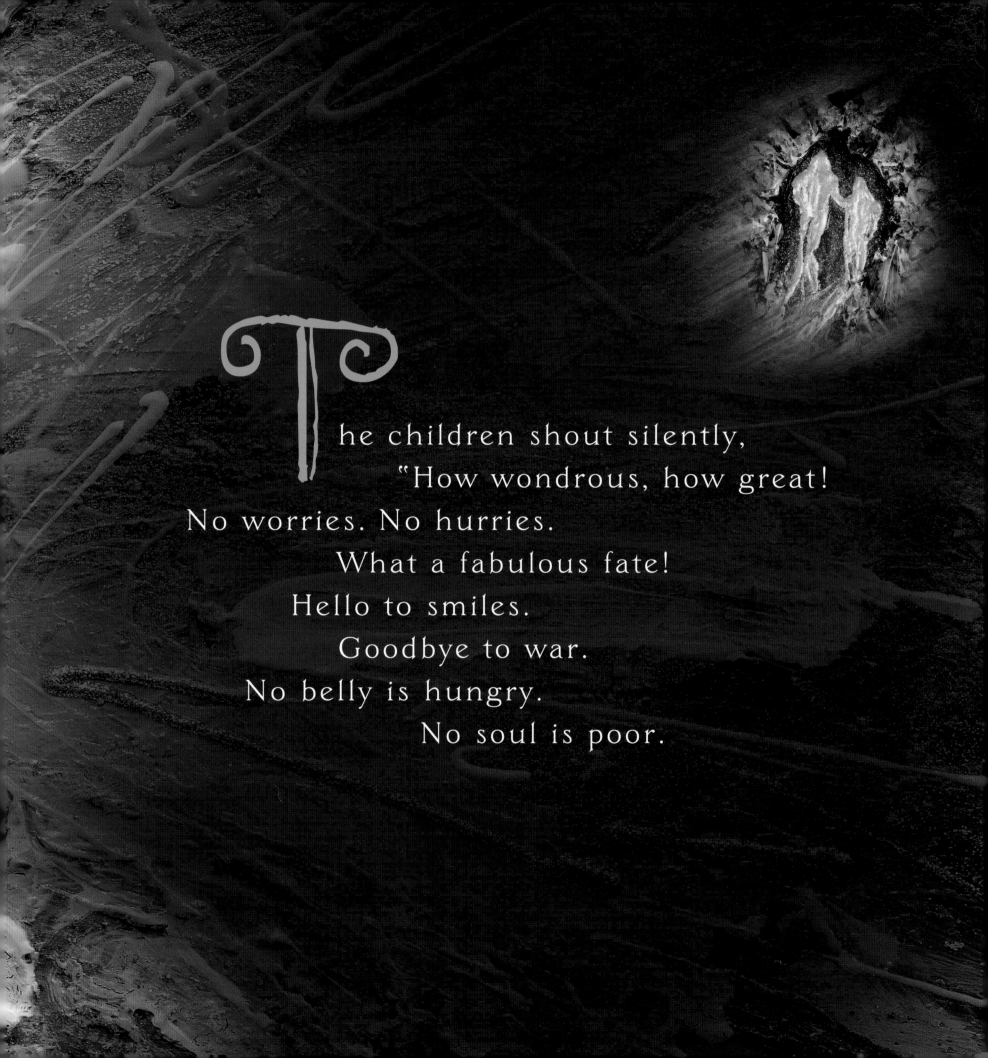

The children shout silently,
"How wondrous, how great!
No worries. No hurries.
What a fabulous fate!
Hello to smiles.
Goodbye to war.
No belly is hungry.
No soul is poor.

"Coins grow in gardens.
Dollars swim sweetened seas.
Children permit parents
To do as they please.

"Cherries peak the mountain tops.
Fudge volcanoes flow.
Trees are made of pretzel sticks
Where ice cream sundaes grow.

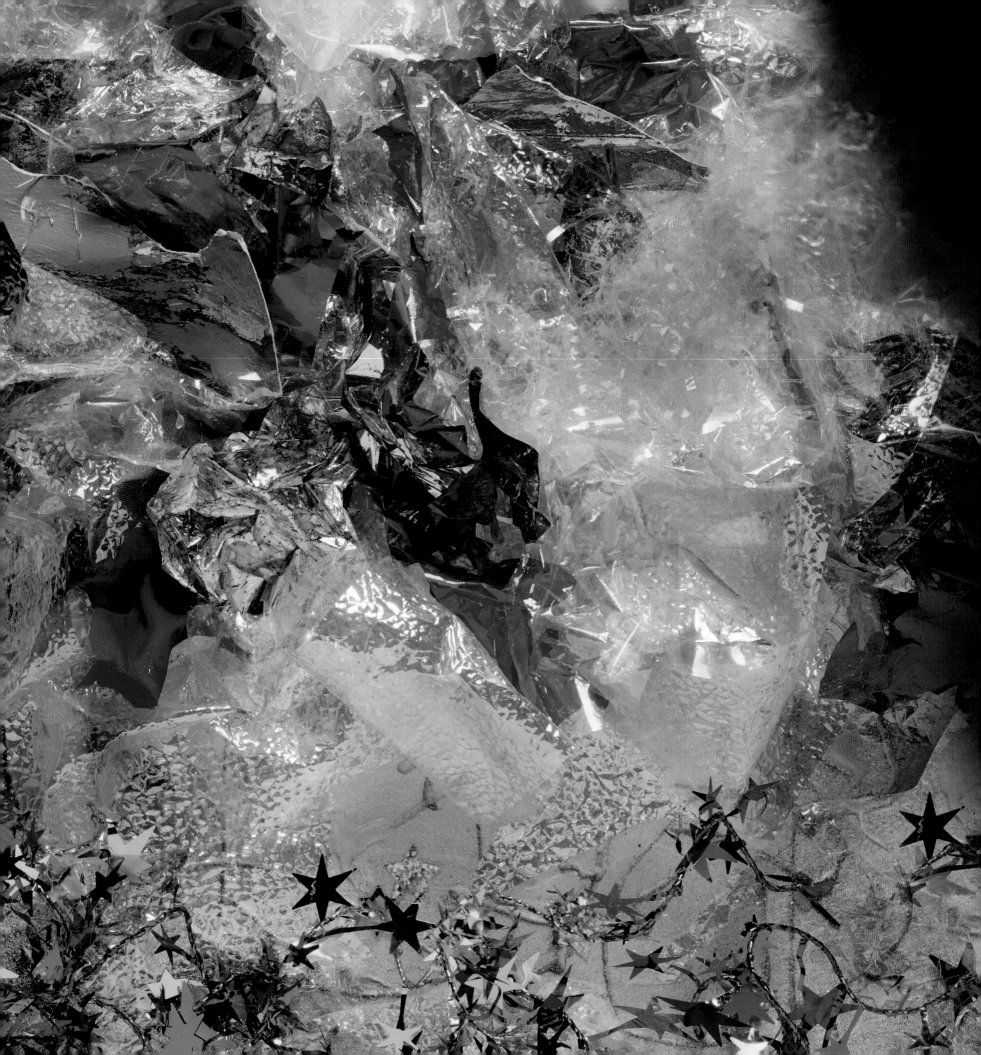

"Air is pure for all to breathe.
A baby never cries.
The young need not grow old.
Nothing living dies.
Oceans form the sky.
Stars form the ground.
All downs are up...
And all ups are down!"

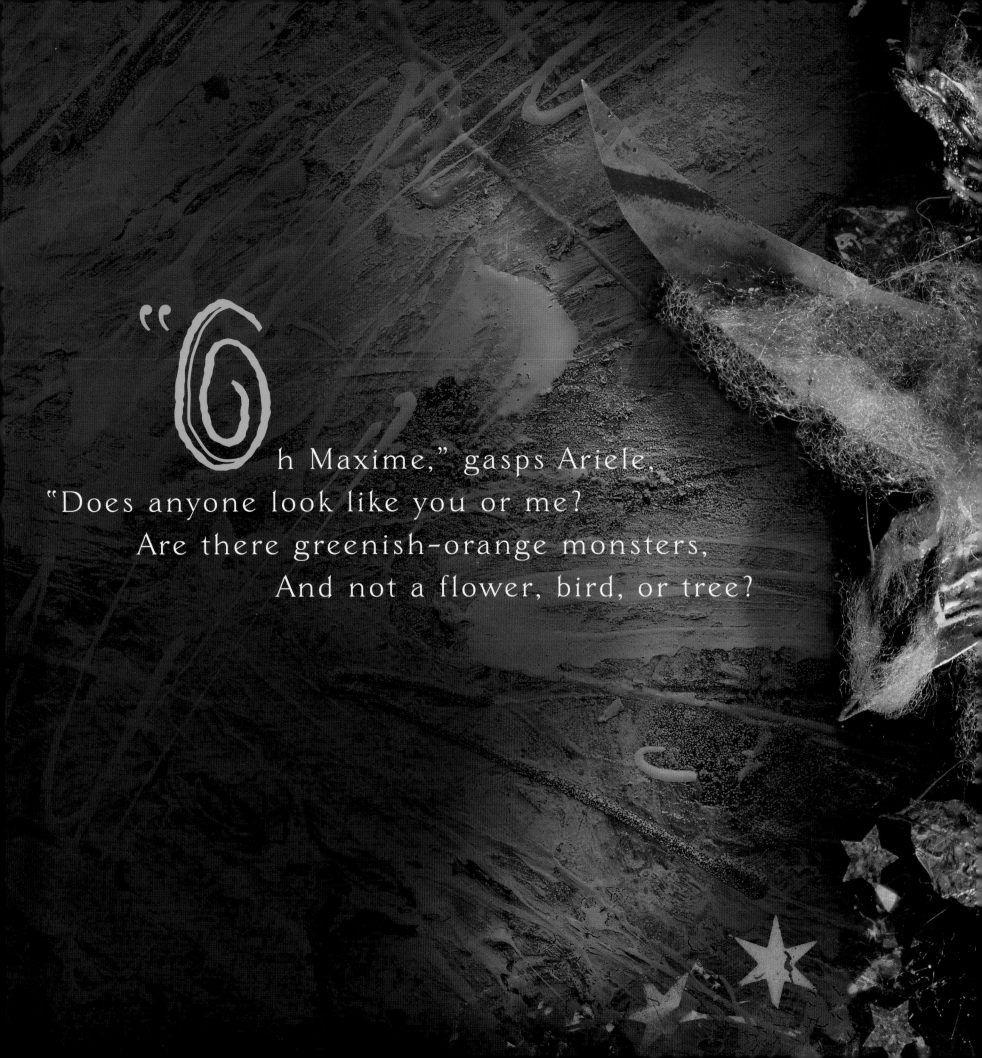

"Oh Maxime," gasps Ariele,
"Does anyone look like you or me?
Are there greenish-orange monsters,
And not a flower, bird, or tree?

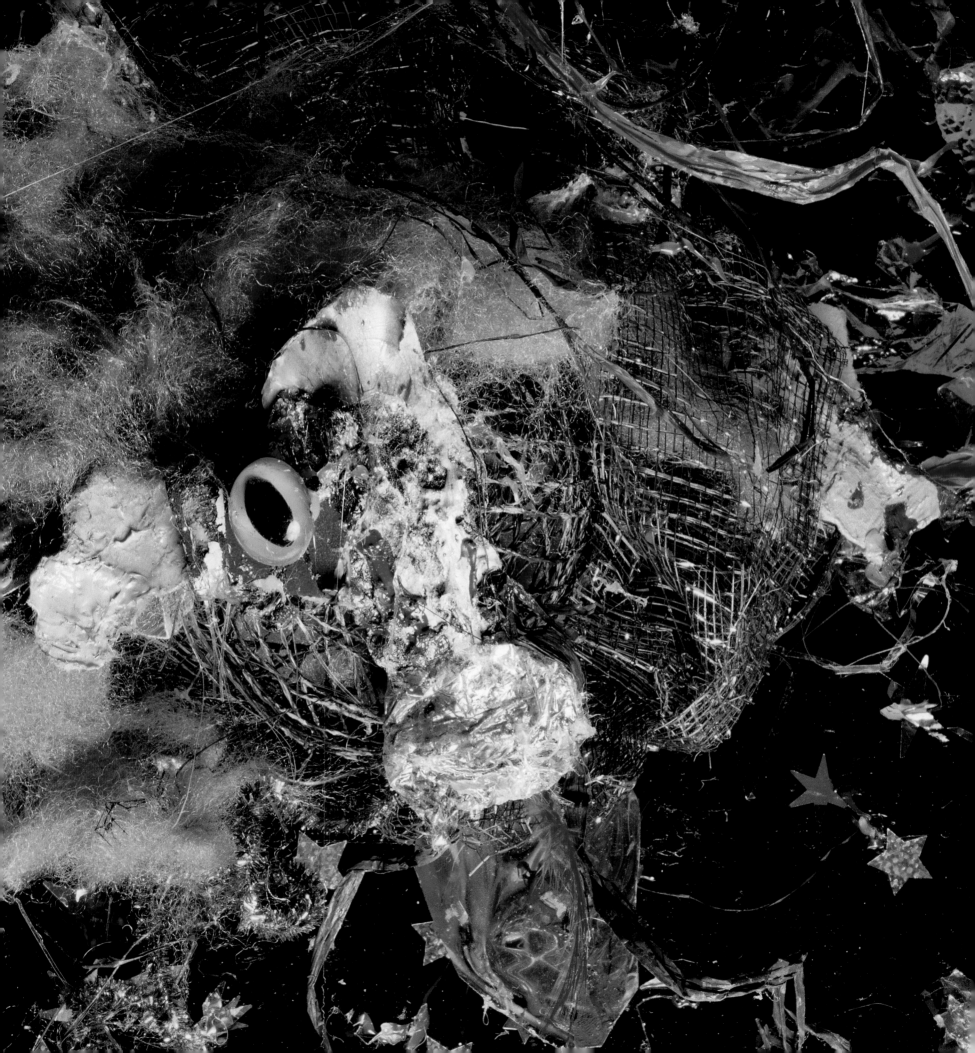

"Suppose there is no love
     Or friendship to ever know.
Perhaps there is just emptiness
     And nothing new can grow!

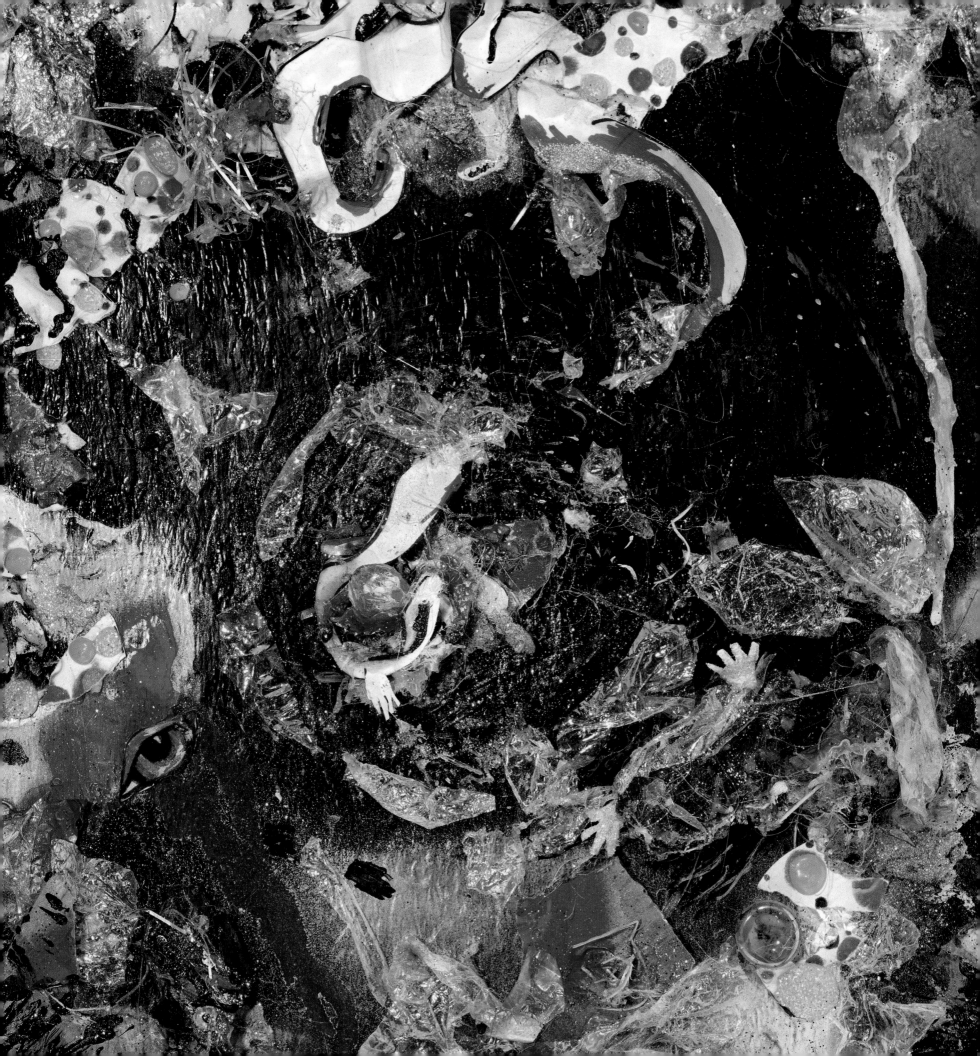

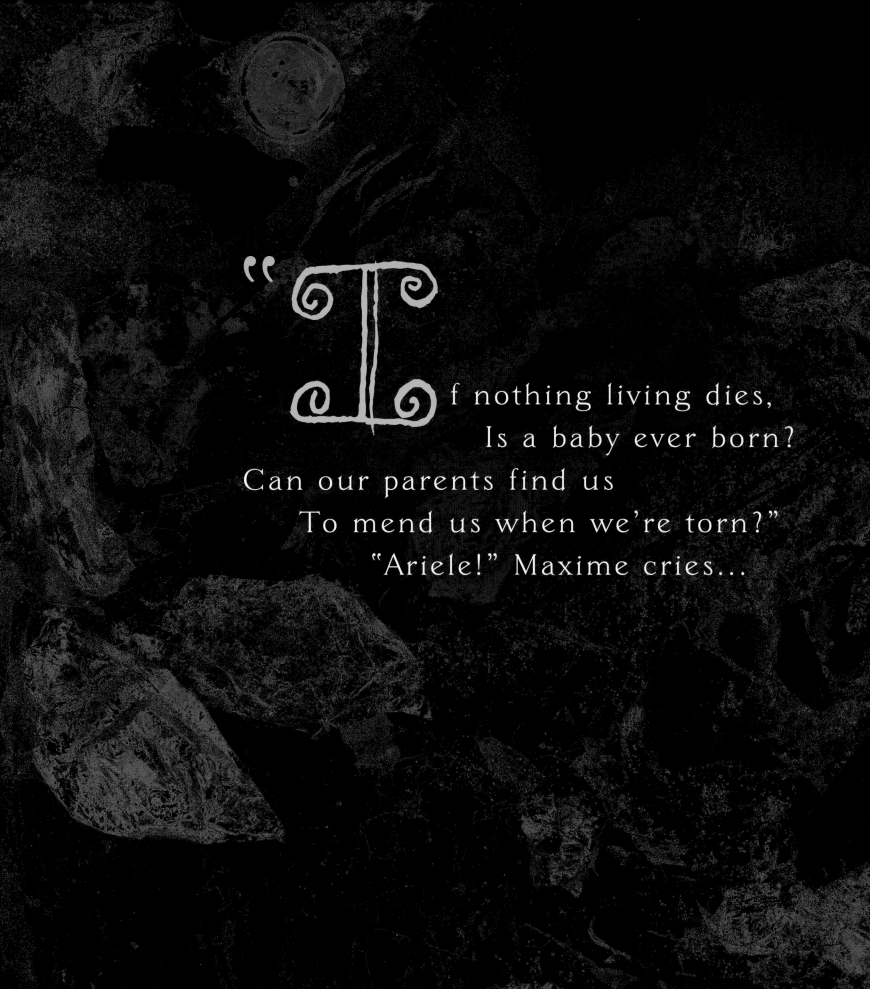

"If nothing living dies,
Is a baby ever born?
Can our parents find us
To mend us when we're torn?"
"Ariele!" Maxime cries...

"If all trues are FALSE

And all falses are TRUE

"Then I cannot be me
And you cannot be you!"

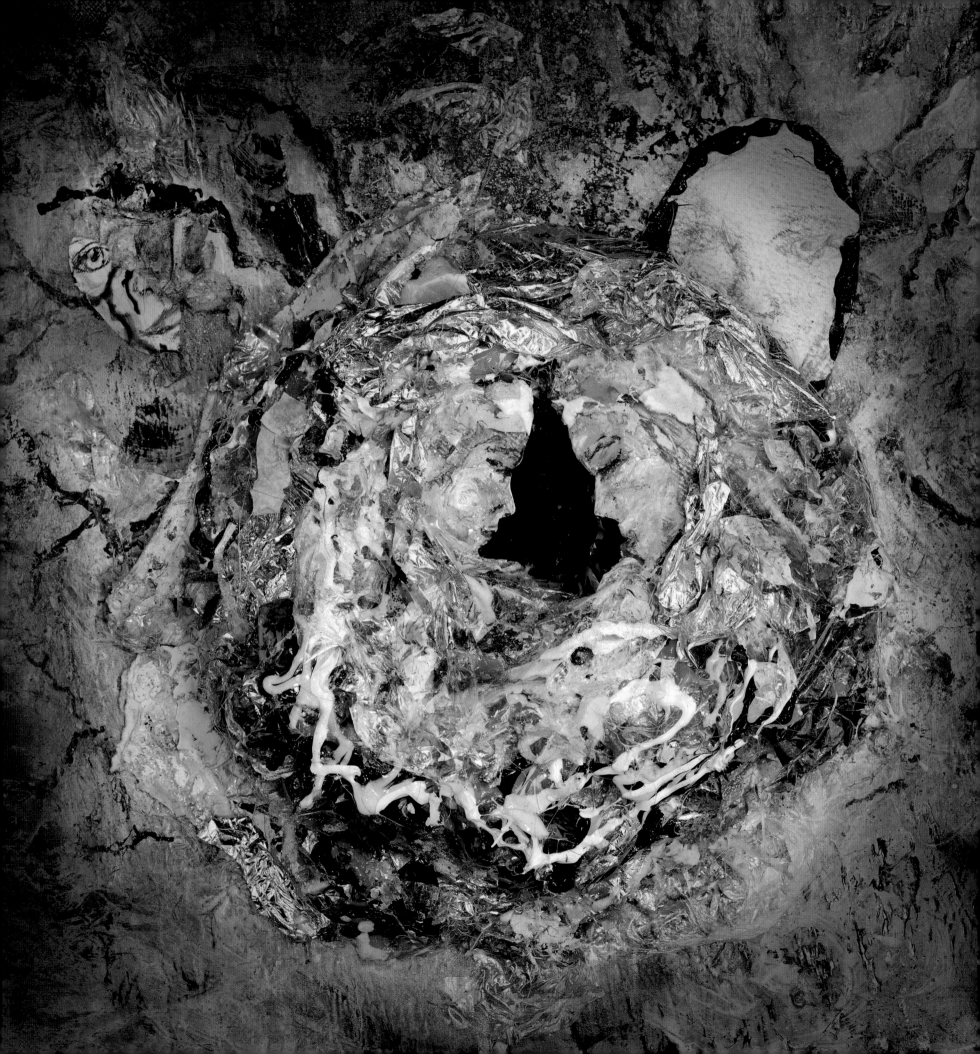

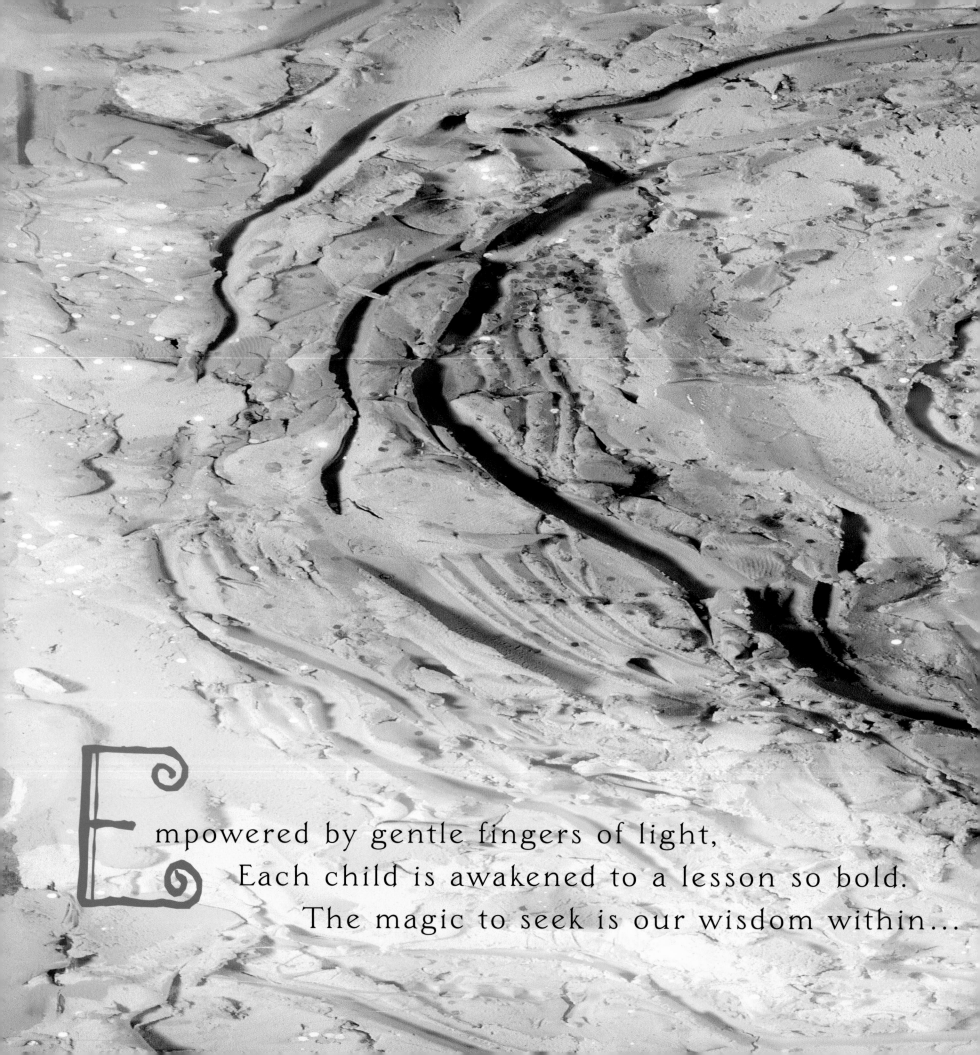

Empowered by gentle fingers of light,
Each child is awakened to a lesson so bold.
The magic to seek is our wisdom within...

is surely not gold!

"Goodbye Zebra-Striped Whale
With the Polka-Dot Tail...
And Pink and Purple Octopus
Igniting our trail...
And the dazzling colors
Which set us asail!"

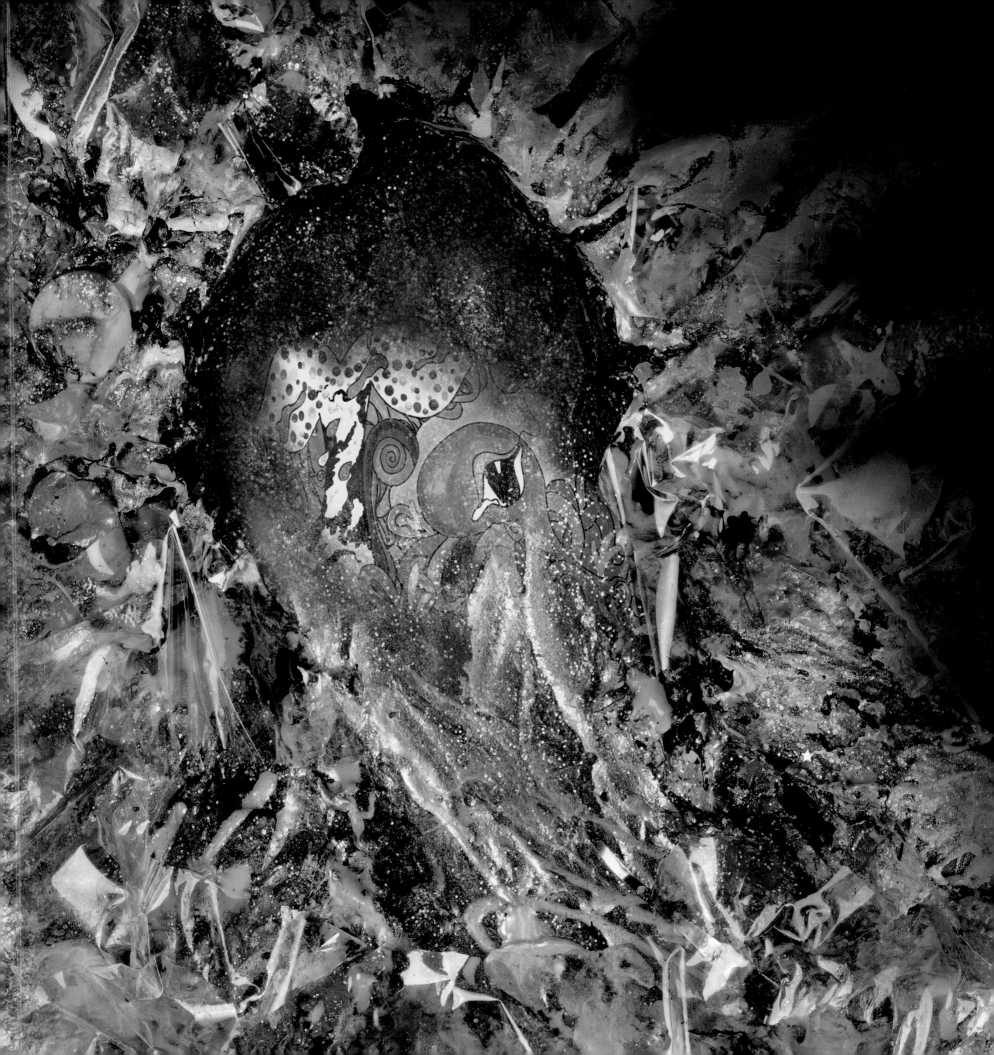

AFTERWORD

I have always admired the knowledge, wisdom and insights of my gregarious and strong protector, my dad, Leon Leigh Faden. When he suddenly died on March 12, 1990, I yearned to comprehend the numerous profound conversations we had shared regarding God … spirituality … nature … religion … the universe … and even death. Inspiration gently unveiled itself in the stream of my cherished memories. Within weeks after my father's passing, verse after verse of *The Zebra-Striped Whale with the Polka-Dot Tail* emerged, granting me peace of mind and renewal of spirit.

In the ongoing process of healing, I have spent almost a decade creating a series of artistic renderings to accompany my poetic journey. The visual interpretations included in this book were prepared from a wide variety of elements including fabric, paper, cellophane, paint, clay, and any other dimensional materials that I could find. Prior to this time, I was unaware that I had the skills of either a writer or an artist.

In honor of my father, Leon Leigh Faden, I rejoice in the culmination of this labor of love — a whimsical tale for the child … in each of us. As a metaphor for life, this spiritual adventure takes us on the ultimate journey to discover the truth within ourselves. Maturity and wisdom, symbolized by the zebra-striped whale with the polka-dot tail and the pink and purple octopus igniting our trail, determine the light of our choices, our paths, and ultimately our destinies.

With every passing moment, the essence of *all that glitters is not gold* pierces our core. From the distraction of our mounting wants, we embark on the journey inward toward peace. With inspiring awe, we quietly surrender to the light of wisdom deep within our soul — for that which we seek, we discover at last, within ourselves.

Only in love and kindness, grace and goodness, mercy and justice,
compassion and solicitude, trust and understanding
and faith can we see the light.

—*Leon Leigh Faden*

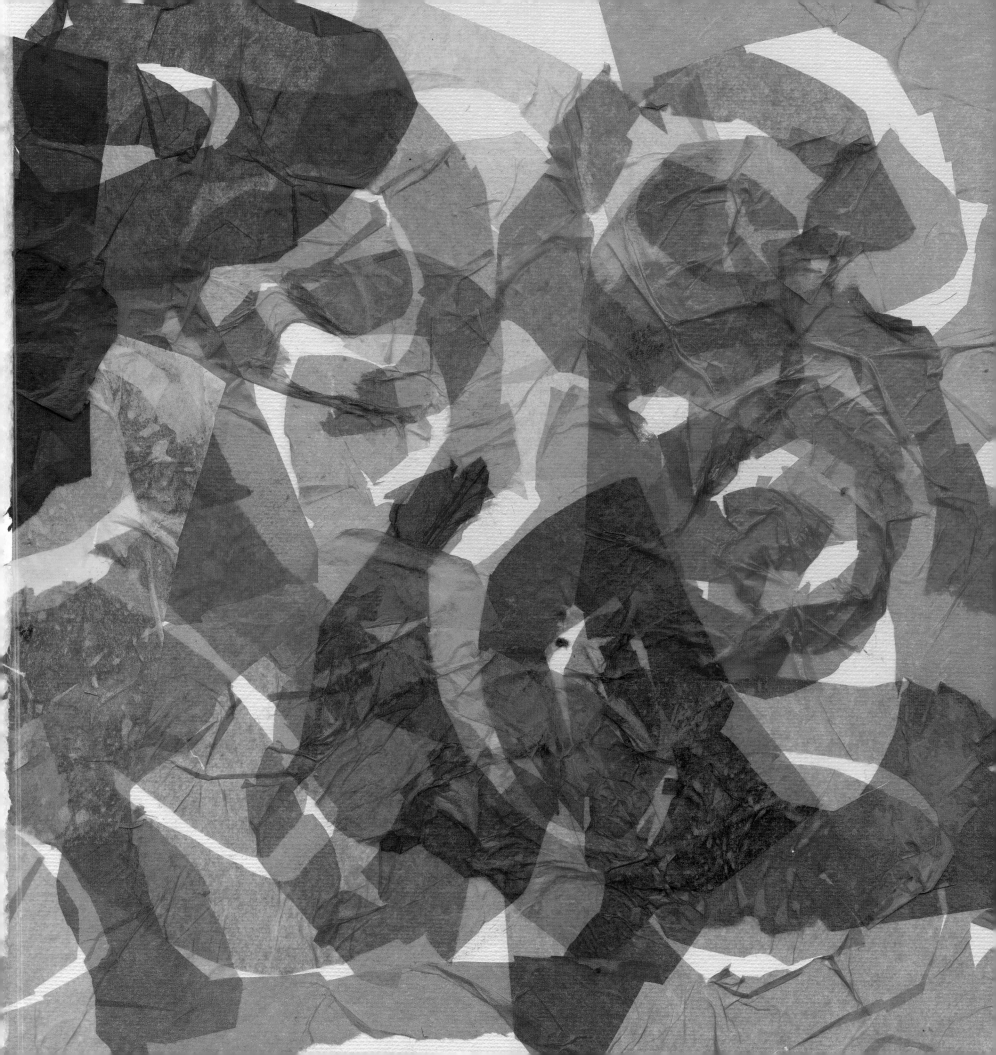